David Fickling Books
presents

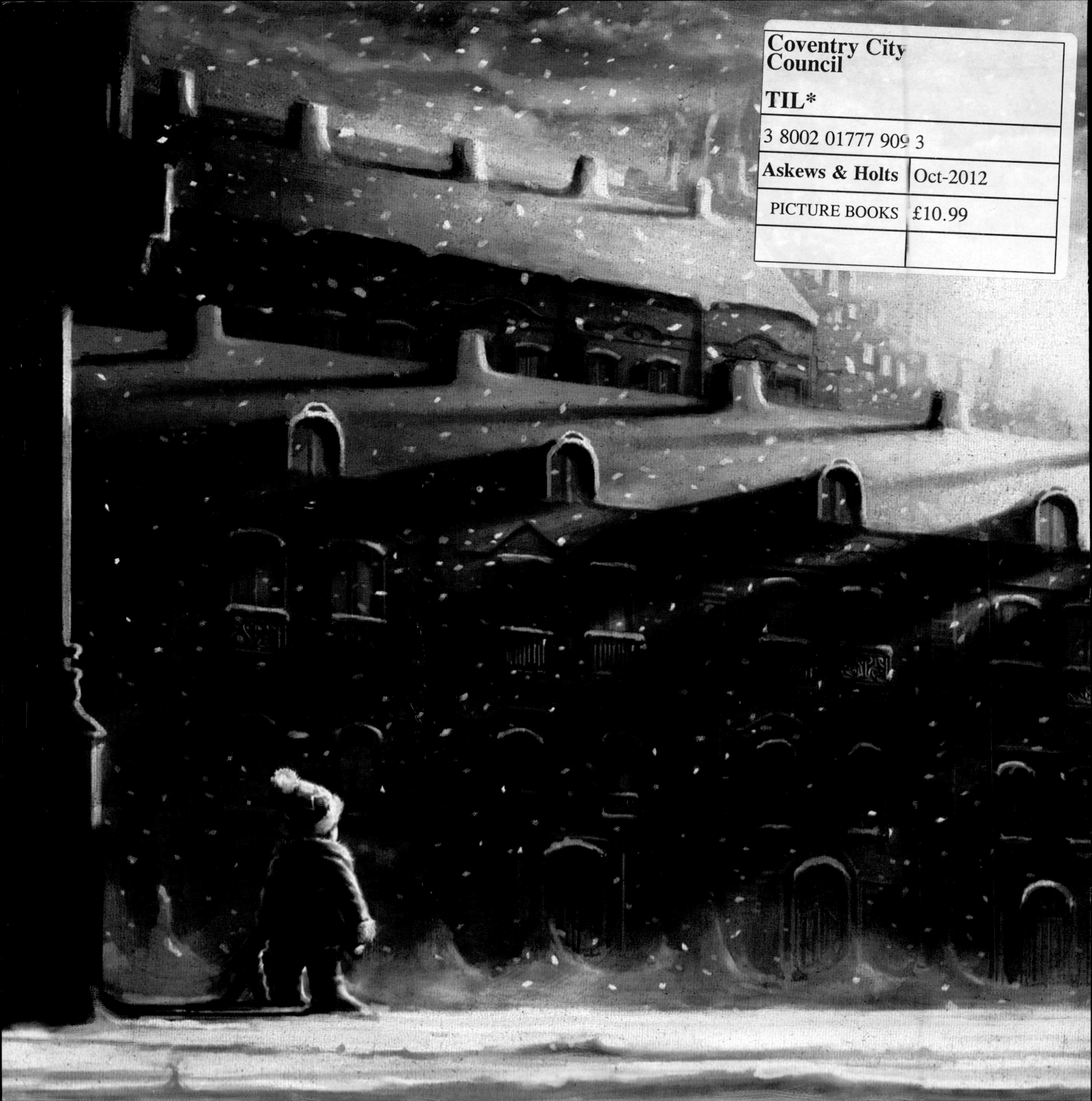

WHEN IT SNOWS

RICHARD COLLINGRIDGE

When it snows . . .

all the cars are stuck and
the train has disappeared.

So, I follow the footprints

until I find a new way
to get around.

I play for the rest of the way

to the place where
the snowmen live.

And when the sun sinks,
I follow a bright light into the dark.

It leads me through the
gloomy forest

where I meet the
Queen of the Poles.

She takes me to a secret place

with tiny fairies that glow.

I see thousands
of elves

and a giant
reindeer as well.

And I can go there
every day . . .

because my favourite
book takes me there.

THE END

WHEN IT SNOWS. A DAVID FICKLING BOOK 978 0 85756 049 0
Published in Great Britain by David Fickling Books,
a division of Random House Children's Books, A Random House Group company

1 3 5 7 9 10 8 6 4 2

This edition published 2012. Copyright © Richard Collingridge, 2012.
The right of Richard Collingridge to be identified as the author of this work has been asserted
in accordance with the Copyright, Designs and Patents Act 1988.
All rights reserved. DAVID FICKLING BOOKS, 31 Beaumont Street, Oxford, OX1 2NP
www.kidsatrandomhouse.co.uk www.totallyrandombooks.co.uk www.randomhouse.co.uk
Addresses for companies within The Random House Group Limited can be found at:
www.randomhouse.co.uk/offices.htm
THE RANDOM HOUSE GROUP Limited Reg. No. 954009

A CIP catalogue record for this book is available from the British Library.
Printed in China.

To Kim and Françoise